DAD JOKES COLORING BOOK

ha-ha-ha

A NOTE TO DAD :

_____

_____

_____

_____

_____

 FOLLOW US AT:

@DADJOKES1 **@DADJOKES01**

WWW.DADJOKESGIFT.COM

Copyright ©DAD JOKES COLORING BOOK All rights reserved. This book or any portion thereof may not be reproduced or used in any manner whatsoever without the express written permission of the publisher except for the use of brief quotations in a book review.
Printed Worldwide
First Printing, 2020

DAD I NEED TO TALK TO YOU ABOUT YOUR PROCRASTINATING.

LET'S TALK ABOUT IT LATER

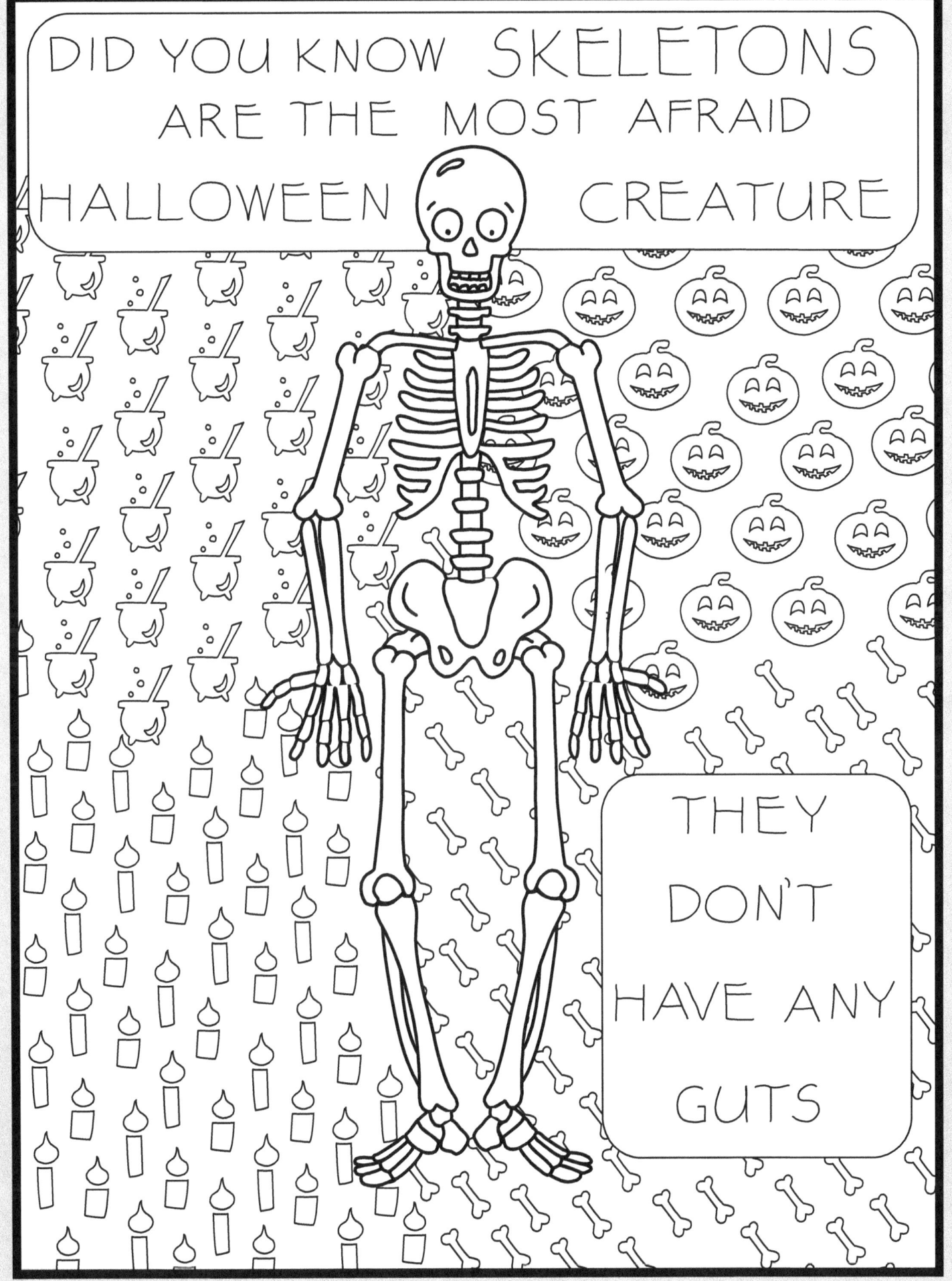

the answer to
this math problem is
zero.

new
equation:
nothing.

DAD I NEED TO TALK TO YOU ABOUT YOUR PROCRASTINATING.

LET'S TALK ABOUT IT LATER

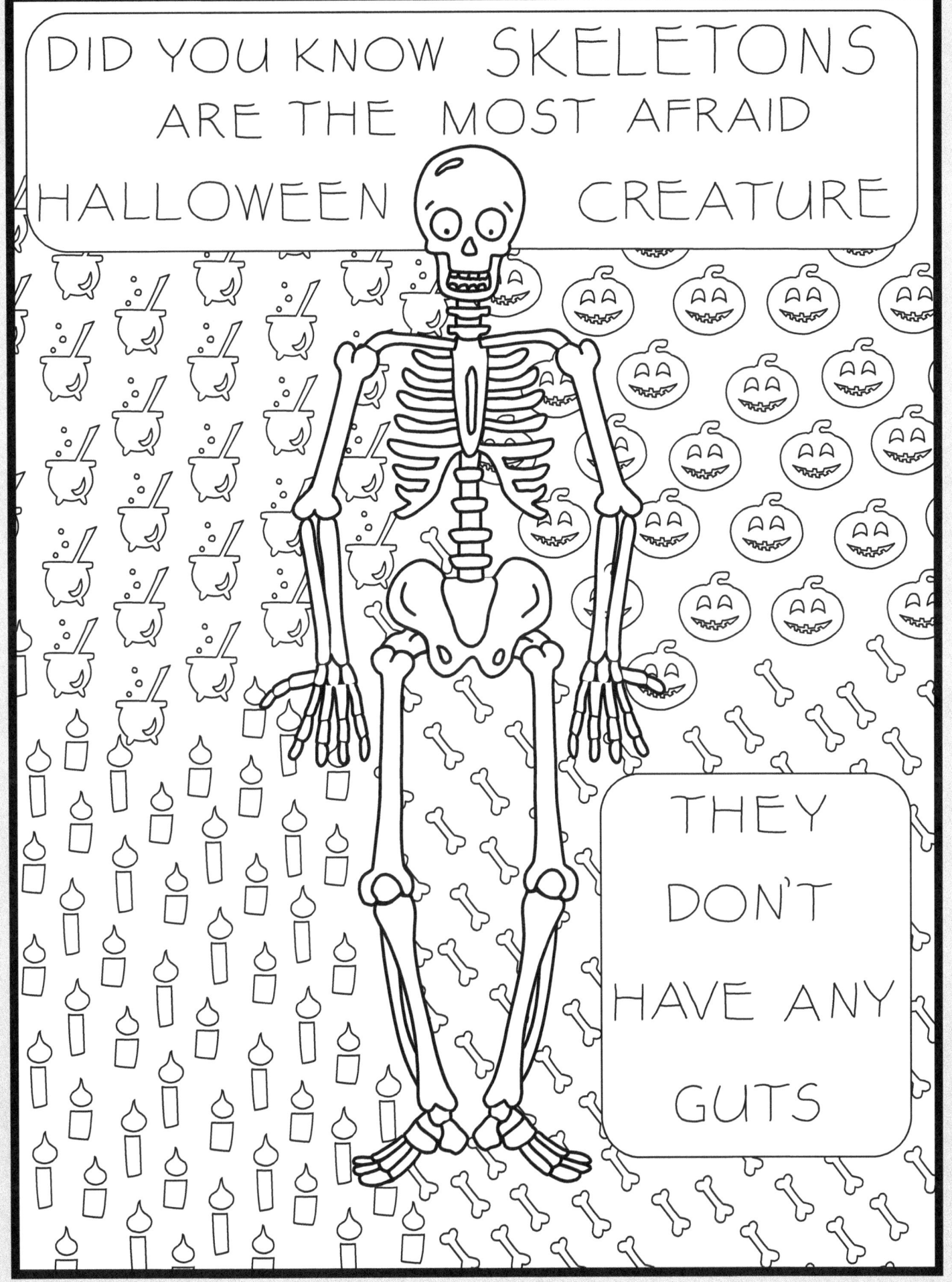

www.ingramcontent.com/pod-product-compliance
Lightning Source LLC
Chambersburg PA
CBHW081120080526
44587CB00021B/3681